FRIENDS FREE LIBRARY
GERMANTOWN FRIENDS LIBRARY
5418 Germantown Avenue
Philadelphia, PA 19144
215-951-2355

Each borrower is responsible for all items
checked out on his/her library card, for
fines on materials kept overtime, and
replacing any lost or damaged materials.

When the sun came out, the jungle was back to normal.
The stripes were on the zebras instead of the lion.
And Chameleon was back to normal too—changing
from brown to green, from green to yellow—all to
match his surroundings.

Suddenly, a clap of thunder roared
through the sky and huge sheets
of rain poured down, washing
the colors off the animals.
Chameleon breathed a sigh of relief.

They chased him to the edge of a cliff.
Trembling, Chameleon closed his eyes,
turned the color of the rocks, and waited ...

Soon all the other animals were complaining too. "Life was much easier with our old colors. Now everything is messed up and it's all your fault, Chameleon! Change us back!" They rushed toward him angrily.

But the next day Lion started complaining. "These colors are a big mistake," he said. "I'm hungry, but I can't even tell the difference between a zebra and a hippo. How am I supposed to recognize my dinner?"

"Lion is right," hissed Snake. "I can't hide in the grass anymore. You can see my bright red skin from a mile away."

"What would you like?" called Chameleon. "Choose your style—striped, polka-dotted, checkered, flowered—any pattern under the sun."

"What a great idea, Chameleon," said the animals.

They all went home colorful and happy. Chameleon was very happy too. He had become the most popular animal in the whole jungle.

"Chameleon's Colors! Bear or Flea—
tell me what color you want to be!"
Chameleon sang as loudly as he could.
The wind carried his voice
throughout the jungle, and soon the
animals began to arrive.

That night, Chameleon stayed up late collecting flowers, fruit, and leaves. He squeezed out their juices and mixed them in little coconut shells. He couldn't wait for morning.

"Day after day, I'm the same old muddy gray," Hippo explained.
"I wish I could be a different color."

"Well, if that is what you really want…" said Chameleon.
He grabbed some pink blossoms, stomped on them, and
splashed the juice all over Hippo.
"That's fabulous!" said Hippo. "Now I'm pink like you!"
Chameleon smiled happily. He had a great idea.

"Oops! Sorry, Chameleon!" Hippo almost stepped on him. "I didn't even see you."

"I know," said Chameleon. "No one *ever* sees me. I'm sick of it."

"I think it would be fun to change colors," said Hippo.

"What?" Chameleon was surprised.

Chameleon was always changing colors. No matter where he went, his skin would change—from brown to green, from green to yellow—all to match his surroundings.

Sometimes even his best friends would walk right by without seeing him. They would think he was a piece of wood, a leaf, a flower, or a stone.

Library of Congress Cataloging-in-Publication Data is available.
A CIP catalogue record for this book is available from The British Library.

ISBN-13: 978-0-7358-1887-3 / ISBN-10: 0-7358-1887-8 (trade edition) 10 9 8 7 6 5 4 3
ISBN-13: 978-0-7358-1882-8 / ISBN-10: 0-7358-1882-7 (library edition) 10 9 8 7 6 5 4 3 2 1
ISBN-13: 978-0-7358-2111-8 / ISBN-10: 0-7358-2111-9 (paperback edition) 10 9 8 7 6 5 4 3 2 1

Printed in Italy

JE
TAS

CHISATO TASHIRO

CHAMELEON'S COLORS

Translated by Marianne Martens

A MICHAEL NEUGEBAUER BOOK

NorthSouth
BOOKS
NEW YORK / LONDON